I Went For Hajj

by Na'ima B. Robert　　　Illustrated by Paula Pang

Note to Parents and Teachers

This book is a purely inspirational, semi-fictional narrative. It describes a personal experience of Hajj from a young child's perspective. It is not a comprehensive guide. The rhyming text serves to create interest for the child as they read/listen to the narrative but it is expected that the parents or teachers will discuss and elaborate further on the concept and rituals of Hajj according to the child's age and level of understanding. This book cannot replace a book of fiqh to prepare an older child or adult for the step-by-step obligations of Hajj according to a particular school of thought.

Points that you may wish to highlight in your discussion with children include:

- Hajj is completed over five days during the month of Dhu'l Hijjah. It is a set of acts of worship as prescribed by Allah and performed by the Prophet Muhammad ﷺ. It is one of the pillars of Islam.

- Ihram is the condition of consecration and the outfit made up of two unsewn pieces of white cloth for men and loose garments for women (may be white but not necessary).

- It can be put on anywhere before reaching the point of Meeqat; a set boundary around Makkah. The pilgrims announce their intention of Hajj at this point and enter into consecration.

- The black stone or hajr al-aswad is built into the south-east corner of the Ka'bah. It is part of the original construction of the Ka'bah carried out by Prophets Ibrahim and Ismail ﷺ .

- The station of Ibrahim is the step-stone used by Prophet Ibrahim ﷺ in the original construction of the Ka'bah. Now housed in a glass enclosure near the Ka'bah.

- Tawaf is the act of going round the Ka'bah while reciting duas/prayers. It is done seven times, counter clockwise and is a compulsory part of Hajj.

- During sa'i pilgrims run seven times between Safa and Marwa as done by Sayyidah Hajar when she was looking for water for her baby, Prophet Ismail عليه السلام. Safa and Marwa are two hillocks located close to the Ka'bah.

- Mina is a desert location around three miles from Makkah. The pilgrims stay in tents here as they perform the rites of Hajj.

- Arafat is a hilly location around nine miles from Makkah where the pilgrims pray on the 9th day of Dhu'l Hijjah as one of the rites of Hajj. The Prophet ﷺ encouraged the pilgrims to spend that day in dua.

- Muzdalifah is midway between Mina and Arafat. The pilgrims spend the night of 9th Dhu'l Hijjah here under the open sky.

- Rami is the symbolic stoning of Shaytan done by throwing pebbles at three large pillars known as the Jamaraat. It is close to Mina and is done over three days – 10th to 13th of Dhu'l Hijjah.

- Men either shave their hair off completely or trim it short marking the end of their Hajj; removal of the state of ihram. Women do not shave their hair instead they trim the bottom of a few locks.

Hajji, hajji,
what did you see?

From the plane
I saw clouds
And the **big,**
blue sea.

7

Hajji, hajji,
what did you wear?

I wore two white sheets
And my shoulder was bare.

Allahu Akbar...

...kbar...

I heard the call
to prayer
As it filled the air.

11

Hajji, hajji,
what did you see?

I saw the
great
mosque
As bright
as can be.

The Ka'aba, the
black stone
And the station
of Ibrahim ﷺ.

12

Hajji, hajji,

what did you do?

14

I made tawaaf seven times
Like the Prophet ﷺ used to.

Hajji, hajji,
what did you see?

The **HILLS** of
Safa and **Marwa**

SAFA

As I ran in between!

Hajji, hajji, where did you go?

18

To a place called Mina

Where the tents
**stand
in
rows.**

Hajji, hajji,
what did you do?

20

I prayed on **Arafat**
Like the Prophet ﷺ would do.

21

Hajji, hajji,
what did you feel?

I felt the
COLD night air

22

When we all went
to **sleep.**

Hajji, hajji,
what did you see?

I saw **stones** being thrown

24

And lots
of hands
and feet.

Hajji, hajji, what did you eat?

I ate chicken, rice and fruit
And on **Eid** we had meat.

Hajji, hajji, what did you see?

I saw men shave their hair

Now I'm as **bald** as can be!

28

Hajji, hajji, what do you know?

My special **Hajj** will stay with me

Wherever I go!

Hajj Mabroor!

Glossary

Arafat – Place where the pilgrims spend the 9th day of Dhu'l Hijjah in prayer and supplication.

Black stone – Cornerstone of Ka'bah; visited during pilgrimage.

Hajj – Pilgrimage to Makkah; fifth pillar of Islam.

Hajji – A Muslim who has completed the pilgrimage to Makkah.

Ihram – State of purification with the intention of Hajj/Umrah marked by the wearing of two unsewn white sheets by men and loose clothing by women.

Jamaarat – Three large pillars near Mina; visited during pilgrimage.

Ka'bah – First house of worship built by Prophets Ibrahim and Ismail ﷺ.

Marwa – One of the two hillocks near the Ka'bah; visited during pilgrimage.